Animal Tales

Collection © 2007 Bayard Canada Books Inc.
Stories and illustrations © authors and illustrators

Publisher: Jennifer Canham
Editorial Director: Mary Beth Leatherdale
Editor: Katherine Dearlove
Production Editor: Larissa Byj
Production Assistant: Kathy Ko

Design Concept: Blair Kerrigan
Designer: Stephanie Olive
Jacket Design: Barb Kelly

Special thanks to Craig Battle, David Field, Angela Keenlyside, Paul Markowski, Sarah Trusty, and Lesley Zimic.

"Little Koi" illustration by Marthe Jocelyn was photographed by Ian Crysler.

We gratefully acknowledge the financial support of the Government of Canada through the Book Publishing Industry Development Program (BPIDP) for our publishing activities.

Conseil des Arts **Canada Council**
du Canada **for the Arts**

Library and Archives Canada Cataloguing in Publication

     Animal tales : favourite stories from Chirp magazine.

ISBN 978-2-89579-174-4

     1. Animals--Juvenile fiction. 2. Children's stories. 3. Short stories, Canadian (English).

PS8323.A5A55 2007   jC813'.0108362   C2007-903243-5

Printed in Canada

Owlkids Publishing
10 Lower Spadina Ave., Suite 400
Toronto, Ontario M5V 2Z2
Ph: 416-340-2700
Fax: 416-340-9769

Publisher of

CHIRP **chickaDEE** **OWL**

www.owlkids.com

Animal Tales

Favourite Stories from Chirp Magazine

Owl kids

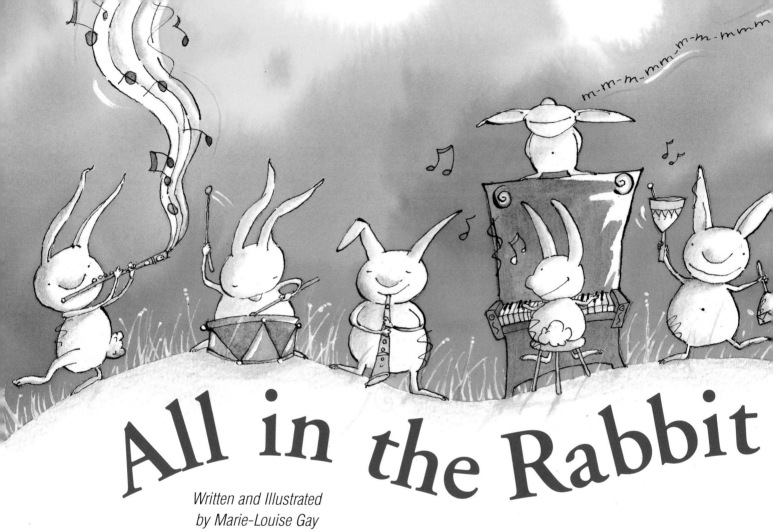

All in the Rabbit

Written and Illustrated
by Marie-Louise Gay

Fifi plays the flute,
Diego pounds the drums,
Oona plays the oboe,
while tiny Hester hum-m-m-ms....

Then there's Emma who is silent,
silent as a mouse.
No one even knows
if Emma's in the house.

Peter plays the piano,
Bella rings the bells,
Trevor plays the tuba,
while little Yasmin ye-l-l-l-ls!!!

Then there's Emma who is quiet,
she doesn't even peep,
Emma is very quiet
'cause all she does is sleep.

Family Orchestra...

Toby plays the trumpet,
Sarah plucks the strings,
Boris plays the bagpipes,
while Sophie's sister **si-i-i-i-ngs.**

But Emma doesn't sing.
She doesn't even roar.
She doesn't play marimbas.
But Emma likes to... **sno-o-o-o-o-re!**

Armadillo's Special Day

Written by Margriet Ruurs
Illustrated by Fil et Julie

Armadillo woke with a jolt.
The sun tickled his tail as it peeked out from under a prickly shrub.

"Hello, Sun!" Armadillo yawned. "Did you know that this is a special day? Today is my birthday!" Armadillo polished his armour and wiggled out of his resting place.

"Today is your birthday?" the sun sang. "I forgot!"

Armadillo frowned. He hoped his other friends wouldn't forget, too.

"Hello, Cactus!" he called, as he noticed a brilliant flower in Cactus's crown. "Are you blooming because it's my birthday?"

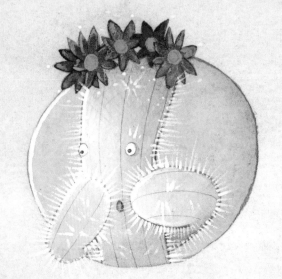

"That's today?" Cactus said prickly. "I plumb forgot!"

"Well," Armadillo thought as he waddled away, "I wonder if everyone else forgot, too!"

Just then, Packrat hopped by.

"Good morning, Packrat! What have you got stuffed into your pockets? Is it something for my birthday?" Armadillo asked hopefully.

"Is that today?" Packrat puffed. "I forgot!" And off he hopped in a great hurry.

Then Snake slithered by with Coyote trotting behind him.

"Do you know what day it is today?" Armadillo called out.

"Is it Thursssssday already?" hissed Snake.

"Cackling cactuses!" Coyote howled. And off they went.

Armadillo stomped his feet. This was not shaping up to be the great day he had imagined. He spotted Lizard, lounging on a rock, flicking her tongue lazily at some flies.

"Can I join you? I need cheering up," Armadillo sniffed.

"I don't have time right now," Lizard lisped. "I'm on my way somewhere. And I'm late! But you can come with me if you want." And off Lizard dashed.

Armadillo began to cheer up. Now at least he would have company. But where had Lizard gone?

"Where are you?" Armadillo hollered. There was no one in sight. Just empty desert. He scratched his scales and waddled around a rock.

"SURPRISE!" All of Armadillo's friends jumped out from behind the rock. Lizard blew her party horn. Cactus waved a bouquet of flowers. Packrat pulled a perfect present out of his pouch and Snake hissed a birthday wisssh.

se!

They had bugs in a bowl and snake cake for a desert dessert. They played Pin the Tail on the Salamander, and Coyote taught them cowboy songs until it was time to go home.

"Thank you for not forgetting my birthday!" Armadillo smiled, just as the sun painted the whole desert orange, just for him. ❧

11

Frank
the Bear

*Written and Illustrated
by David McPhail*

Frank worked at a bank. It was a big bank on the edge of a forest. Frank's job was to guard the money. Frank liked being a bank guard. He got to wear a fancy uniform. The uniform was red with gold buttons. There was also a big blue hat. Part of Frank's job at the big bank was to take money to smaller banks when they ran out. Frank would put the bags of money in a wheelbarrow and deliver them.

One day Frank was taking money to a little bank on the far side of the forest. He loaded the money into the wheelbarrow and started out. Frank was about halfway there when he was set upon by a band of thieves. There was a fox, a couple of rabbits, and a crow blocking the path.

"Give us all the money," the thieves told Frank.

"I won't," said Frank. "I'm delivering it to the bank and I'm running late. Now get out of the way!" But the thieves wouldn't budge.

"Hand over the money," the fox insisted. "If you don't, we'll be forced to take it from you."

Frank nearly laughed. If he wanted to, he could stuff every one of this ragged bunch into his coat pocket. Instead he set the wheelbarrow down and started to walk away. "It's all yours," Frank called over his shoulder.

The fox grabbed the wheelbarrow handles and tried to lift. "*Oommpfh!*" he grunted. But the wheelbarrow was so filled with bags of money that it wouldn't budge. "Here, give me a hand!" the fox said to the rabbits. Even with the rabbits' help, the wheelbarrow didn't move at all.

Meanwhile, Frank was watching the thieves from behind a tree. He had only pretended to leave. "Stand back," the crow said to the fox and the rabbits. "I'll handle this!" She took a bag of money in her beak and tried to fly. She managed to get as far as the tree Frank was hiding behind before she crashed. Frank stepped out from behind the tree.

"Let me give you a hand," he said to the thieves. "Which way?" The thieves headed off down the path and Frank followed along, pushing the wheelbarrow. "Why do you want this money?" Frank asked, after they had gone a little way.

"To buy stuff," replied one of the rabbits, "like people do."

"But what do you need to buy?" Frank went on. "Food?"

"No," said the rabbit, "we have all the food we want right here in the forest."

"A new house then?" said Frank.

"I can have a new house any time I want it," said the fox. "I just find a hollow tree and move right in."

"A trip, maybe," said Frank, "to some far-off place?"

"Not me," said the other rabbit. "I like it too much right here!"

"How about new clothes?" Frank said. "Perhaps a pretty dress for crow."

"You must be kidding," said the crow. "Nothing could be prettier than my fine shiny feathers."

"Well," said Frank, "you must want the money for something!" The thieves huddled and whispered amongst themselves.

"We don't want the money, after all," the fox said to Frank. "You keep it."

"There's nothing we want to buy," said one of the rabbits.

"There's nothing we need," said the other.

"It's too heavy, anyway," said the crow.

"If you're sure," said Frank.

"We're sure," said the thieves.

"Then I'd better get going," said Frank, "or I'll surely be late." And Frank walked away pushing the wheelbarrow as the thieves waved goodbye. 🐾

Little Koi

*Written and Illustrated
by Marthe Jocelyn*

Little Koi lived in a pond in the garden where Matsuko played every afternoon. Matsuko liked to sprinkle the water with crumbled rice cakes.

"Here, Little Koi. See what I have for you?" he murmured. Little Koi swam up quickly. Matsuko let his fingertips dangle in the water. Little Koi kissed them in his hurry for a snack.

One day, a leaf drifted down from the cherry tree
and sailed across the pond. It was the first leaf of many,
showing that the change of seasons was near.

"Oh, Little Koi," sighed Matsuko. "What will become
of you, now that winter is coming? What happens when
the surface of the pond turns to ice?"

Little Koi kept nibbling, seeming not to worry.
His fins danced as if blown by an underwater breeze.

One morning, Matsuko awoke
to see the garden dusted with snow.
He hurried to feed Little Koi,
who ate only a few crumbs before
disappearing in the reeds.

"Where do you go?" Matsuko
wondered. "How deep is the
bottom?"

Only a few nights later, winter
arrived with a blast, freezing the
water in Little Koi's pond. Matsuko
tapped the ice with a stick, sending
a message to his friend Little Koi.

"Hello? Little Koi? Are you safe?"
He hoped to see an orange shadow
flit below the ice.

As the weeks went by, Matsuko
spent his afternoons painting pictures
of Little Koi.

"Is he still alive?" Matsuko asked
his father.

"Wait for spring," his father replied.

18

And sure enough,
in the spring, when the
shining sun melted away
the ice, Little Koi darted up
to greet Matsuko as if they had
been playing only yesterday.

To celebrate, Matsuko made a balloon carp,
a *koi-nburi*, that looked just like his friend.
It swam against the breeze in the garden over
Little Koi's pond.

Tracy the Tractor

Written by Shawn Benjamin

Illustrated by Holli Conger

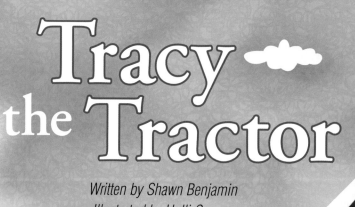

cock-a-doodle-doo

I'm Tracy the Tractor,
my day's just begun.
The rooster is crowing,
there's work to be done.

Rolling out of the barn,
with a puff from my stack,
small wheels in the front,
big wheels in the back.

My trailer's hooked on
and filled up with feed.
I can carry the food
that the animals need.

The chickens eat seeds,
the cows chew on hay,
and the pigs will enjoy
a sloppy buffet.

Connie the Combine
is tooting her horn.
She's out in the field,
she's cutting the corn.

I steer by the stable
to see all the horses,
running and leaping
through high-jumping courses.

toot
toot

21

I hear someone yell
from the end of the farm,
and I see Farmer Brown,
he's waving his arm.

Farmer Brown's driven off
in his little old truck,
but the road is too mucky,
and now he is stuck.

I race out to help him
as fast as I can.
I'm Tracy the Tractor,
your friend in a jam.

So we tie up a rope
to the truck in the guck.
I haul and I pull
till the truck is unstuck.

With one final heave
and one great big pull,
I yank the truck free,
I'm as strong as a bull.

With my day nearly done,
I count up the sheep,
then I go hit the hay,
and fall right asleep.

Spike and Fluffy
Get Dressed Up

*Written and Illustrated
by Roslyn Schwartz*

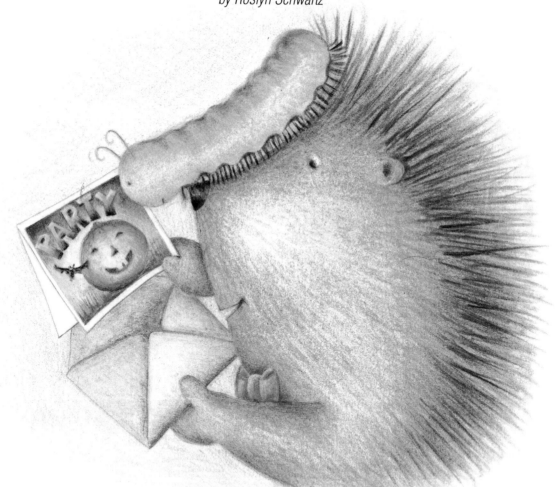

"Look," said Spike the hedgehog to his friend Fluffy the caterpillar. "We've been invited to a party. It's a Halloween party. That means we can dress up. I love dressing up, don't you?"

"I don't know," said Fluffy. "I've never dressed up before. Is it hard?"

"Oh no," said Spike. "It's easy." And he opened the dressing-up basket.

"I know what I'm going to be," said Spike. "I'm going to be a rabbit. What do you think?" And he hopped around the room — **Boinga Boinga**!

"Great," said Fluffy. "You look just like a rabbit. Now let me see, what am I going to be...."

Boinga
Boinga!

25

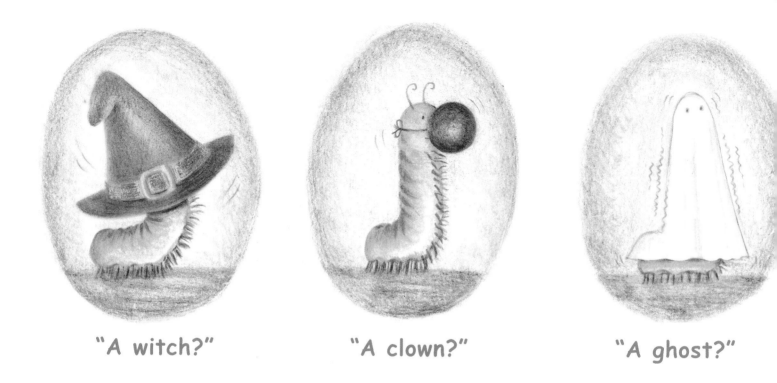

"A witch?" "A clown?" "A ghost?"

"Hmm," said Fluffy. "This is harder than I thought."
Then all of a sudden he saw an orange sock and a green
feather duster. "Aha!" he said.

"I know what I'm going to be. I'm going to be a carrot."

"What do you think?"

"Perfect!" said Spike. "You look good enough to eat."

"Will we win a prize?" said Fluffy.

"I'm sure we will," said Spike. And off they went, through the forest, to the party.

Letter from Grandma's

Written by Gary Barwin
Illustrated by Renée Mansfield

Dear Mom and Dad,

I have been visiting Grandma all week and I have a question. Do you think Grandma is a ? Her house is by itself in the just like in a fairy tale. It isn't made of candy but there is everywhere. Grandma feeds me and lots and lots of . I think she's trying to fatten me up.

Grandma has a just like a witch. She carries a stick everywhere. Maybe it's a magic . Her dress is black and she wears . Spooky, her , is black, too. He stares at me wherever I go.

Today Grandma let me sweep with her 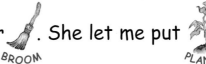 . She let me put  from the

garden into a big 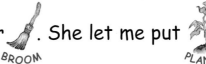 on the .

Then Grandma put on running shoes and took her and we went for a

walk by the river. Grandma made skip across the river. She whistled

like a .

It feels like there is magic around when I stay at Grandma's.

Do you think she is a ? Because if she is,

I want to be a witch, too!

Love, Rudi

The Chipmunk Family's Winter Fun

Written by Celia Barker Lottridge
Illustrated by Clyde Henry

It was winter, a time for chipmunks to sleep. But Acorn was having trouble sleeping.

"It's cold and dark outside," Acorn's mom said. "We're cozy in our hole under the pine tree. It's time to go to sleep!"

Acorn tried and tried. But he wanted to see the dark. He wanted to feel the cold.

"I just can't sleep," he said.

"Do you want some seeds to nibble on?" his mom asked.

"No," said Acorn. "I want to see the dark and feel the cold, and then I'll go to sleep!"

"All right," said Mom. "You may stick your head out of
our tree hole. You'll see the dark and feel the cold. But don't set
one foot outside. Promise?"

"I promise," said Acorn.

He crept around his sisters and brothers to the little tunnel
that led to the outside. He could smell a fresh, cool smell.
"Winter," he thought, as he stuck his head out into the night air.

"Whew!" The cold nearly took his breath away. But it wasn't
dark. It was bright and glittery. There was whiteness everywhere.
"Come quick," Acorn shouted. "It's not dark. It's bright. It's light."

31

Everyone woke up and crowded around the tree hole.

"The moon is shining on the snow," Acorn's dad said.

"Can we go out? Please?" begged the children.

"We'll all go," Mom said. And she led the rush out of the hole.

Dad showed the children how to make a sled out of a dry leaf and slide down the roots of the tree. Mom showed them how to make snow angels. No one had to show them how to throw snowballs and dive into heaps of fluffy snow.

After a while Acorn said, "Winter isn't always dark, but it is cold."

"You're right," said Mom. "And soon it will be dark. The moon is setting. Back into the hole everyone! We'll have some seeds to eat."

They tumbled in and snuggled up into heaps of dry pine needles until they were warm. They nibbled their snack and chattered about their winter adventure.

Then Acorn yawned. "Playing together in the snow was fun. But winter is good for sleeping, too." And he was the first to fall asleep.

Musical Mice

Written and Illustrated
by Maryann Kovalski

Seven little mice lived on seven separate floors in an old, brick building. Melvin lived on the top floor. He practised his tuba every Monday night. He loved Monday nights more than any other night of the week. Tess, who lived below him, did not feel the same.

On Monday night Tess liked a nice hot cup of cocoa and a book. But with the noise that came from Melvin above, Tess could not hear herself think!

"Would it be so hard for Melvin to practise on Tuesday nights when I play my drums? I wouldn't hear a thing. My Tuesday nights are so perfect."

But perfection for Tess was a disaster for Wendel, her neighbour below.

Every Tuesday night Wendel had his old mother over for dinner and a quiet chat.

"I can't hear a word you say, Wendel dear, what with that drumming upstairs! Couldn't she do it on Wednesday nights when you practise your opera singing? You're so loud, her drums wouldn't trouble you at all."

"That's true," Wendel said, "I'm not troubled by anyone or anything on any Wednesday night."

Trudy, who lived below Wendel, was very troubled indeed every Wednesday night. That was the night she dusted her delicate glass figurines. Wendel's singing was so loud that at least one shattered every Wednesday night.

"Boo hoo," cried Trudy as she glued the horn back on her unicorn. "Why can't Wendel sing on Thursday nights when I practise my piano duets. When I get going, no one would hear Wendel — or anything else!"

Nobody knew this better than Frank, who lived below Trudy. On Thursday nights Frank hosted his weekly staring contests. The group required absolute quiet but Trudy's duets made that unlikely. When she hit the first chord, Frank always blinked and lost the game. "Why can't she play on Friday nights?" grumbled Frank as he served cheese puffs to his guests.

"My tap dancing group would never be bothered by the clinking of a few piano keys. When we start tapping we wouldn't hear an earthquake!"

Serena, downstairs, would certainly agree with that. Her Friday night card games were a shambles with Frank's tap dancers banging above them. The thumping was so loud, the cards bounced off the table.

"They couldn't dance on Saturday night when we practise our trombones?" Serena cried.

"I must have a visit with wise, old Seth who lives downstairs on the ground floor. I will visit him in the morning."

"What is wrong, poor Serena?" asked Seth when he opened the door the next day to find Serena wailing on his welcome mat. He invited her in and she told him all about it. When she was finished, Seth nodded.

Each morning that week he'd been visited by someone in the building. Frank came to his door the night before to complain about Trudy, who was there just before him to grouse about Wendel, who had just about had it with Tess, who had little good to say about Melvin.

Seth stroked his beard and thought hard.

Later that day Serena met with Frank, who then talked with Trudy, who phoned up Wendel, who wrote a note to Tess, who ran into Melvin on the stairs.

The next Saturday night, and all that followed, the mice gathered their instruments, put on their dancing shoes, warmed up their singing voices, and made for the roof for a party. Everyone came. Everyone except Seth, who closed his windows, drew his curtains, crawled into his chair, and had a nice, long nap. 🐱

First Day Back

Written by Sharon Jennings
Illustrated by Ruth Ohi

Tommy glared at the poached eggs on his plate. "I hate poached eggs," he said.

"Since when?" asked his mother. "Tommy, it's the first day of school. You have to eat a healthy breakfast."

Tommy sighed. He poked at his egg until the yellow oozed out. He mushed it all around and covered the mess with toast.

"I don't want to go to school," he said. "I want to stay home and watch my favourite show."

"That was last year, Tommy," answered his mother. "You're in grade one now. You're growing up." She kissed the top of his head.

"I don't want to grow up," Tommy declared and stomped upstairs.

He scowled at the new clothes on his bed. The shorts weren't ripped like the ones he wore all summer. They had that stinky, new smell, and when he put on his new shirt, the label was scratchy and rubbed his neck. His shoes were too clean and rubbed his heels.

"I like my old clothes," he said.

"Your old clothes don't fit any more," his mother explained. "You've grown." Then she handed him his knapsack. "I've packed your lunch," she said.

"Lunch!" Tommy groaned. He'd forgotten he had to stay at school all day long.

39

Tommy walked behind his mother the whole way to school. He got as much dirt as he could on his new shoes. His mother waved and said hello to lots of people. Tommy kept his head down except once. That was when he stuck out his tongue when he passed David's house. David was big and mean and called Tommy "pipsqueak" and "squirt."

And then he saw the school. This year Tommy had to go in a different entrance, and he wasn't in nice Mrs. Rawecki's class. This year he had Mr. Singh and he had to sit at a desk in a chair, and grade ones hardly ever got to sit on the carpet or play with toys. He knew this because David's sister said so. She said grade one was hard and Mr. Singh was mean.

Tommy said goodbye to his mother at the classroom door and turned to go in. Lots of kids were already there. But they weren't sitting at the desks.

They were sitting on the carpet in the middle of the room. Then Tommy saw two couches and shelves of books and a box of building blocks and an aquarium and a hamster cage. Tommy started to smile. Maybe grade one wasn't so bad. Then he saw David.

"Hey, shorty!" called David, jumping up. And a wonderful thing happened. Tommy was looking down at David! He was taller than David! Tommy had grown. He had grown a lot. The two boys stared at each other. Tommy thought of all the wonderful, terrible names he could call David to make him feel bad.

But before he could say anything, David smiled. "Wow, Tommy," he said. "You're a giant!" Then Tommy smiled, too, and didn't call David a name after all. He sat down on the carpet beside him. Tommy knew he wasn't a giant. But he did feel very grown up. 🐾

41

Two Heads are Better

Millie and Willie
live high in the trees.
They hang from their toes
and their tails and their knees.

They both like to win
whenever they play.
And they both like to have
their very own way.

Millie, one morning, said,
"Tag would be fun."
"Not it!" Willie cried,
and he started to run.

He dashed along branches
and raced up a tree.
"I'm faster," he boasted.
"You'll never catch me."

He scooted and skittered
and scrambled and stumbled.
He wobbled and tottered,
then suddenly, tumbled...

Down past iguanas
and sloths and macaws.
Past toucans and porcupines
licking their paws.

Than One

Written and Illustrated
by Eugenie Fernandes

He fell to the dark
undercover below,
where jaguars and tapirs
and ocelots go.

Millie ran after him,
swooping and leaping.
She zoomed through the vines
where boas were sleeping.

Past kinkajous creeping,
and butterflies flitting.
And down to the bushes
where Willie was sitting.

"Oh, Willie!" said Millie,
"I hope you're okay."
"Yes, I am," he replied,
And I still want to play."

"I didn't get hurt,
Not at all. Not one bit."
Millie patted his shoulder.
"Oh, good! Then you're it."

Millie hurried away.
"You'll never catch me.
I'm faster than you.
No one's faster than me."

But then, Millie stopped.
And Willie stopped, too.
They heard a strange sound.
What on earth should they do?

They looked all around,
and were very surprised
when they found a young girl
with tears in her eyes.

"My teddy bear fell
in the lake, and before
I was able to grab him,
he floated from shore."

"Don't worry," said Willie.
"I'm clever and quick.
I'll rescue the bear."
Then he picked up a stick.

But try as he might,
He could not reach the teddy.
"Don't worry," said Millie,
"I'm brave and I'm steady."

"I know how to swim,
I'll save him for you."
Millie jumped in the water,
But then she saw two...

44

Giant 'gators beside her
and two underneath.
They were grinning and snapping
their terrible teeth.

Quick as she could,
Millie raced to the shore.
"I'm not going swimming
in there anymore!"

"We can help," Willie said.
"I'm sure that we can."
So they thought, and they talked,
and came up with a plan.

They hung by their tails
and their toes and their knees.
And they picked up the bear,
with the greatest of ease.

What a great save!
What a team! What a pair!
Together they rescued
the little girl's bear.

Some days two monkeys
just want to have fun.
But some days two heads
can be better than one.

Martin Takes the Train

Written by Jane Barclay

Illustrated by Rogé

Martin and his mother were taking the train to visit Aunt Lulu. Martin was excited because he'd never been on a train before. He slid across the seat and looked out the big window.

"All aboard," sang the conductor.

The cars jerked forward and the wheels squeaked on the rails.

"*Choo-chooo,*" went the train as it started with a groan.

"*Boo-hoo,*" cried a granny as she blew kisses from the platform.

"*Ya-hoo!*" said Martin as he bounced up and down.

The train clattered across a metal bridge when suddenly it got dark.

"*Choo-chooo,*" went the train as it crept through the tunnel.

"Coo-coo," called the pigeons from their nest in the rafters.

"Ya-hoo!" said Martin as he pretended to be a ghost.

Soon they came to a crossing. Lights flashed, bells clanged, and cars stopped. Martin could see a lady and a baby on a bike.

"Choo-chooo," went the train as they crawled past the gates.

"Goo-goo," gurgled the baby from her seat on the bike.

"Ya-hoo!" said Martin as he made a silly face.

On and on they rode. Soon the
houses they were passing changed into
farms. Families of black-and-white cows lay
underneath the trees in the shade.

"*Choo-chooo,*" went the train as it sped past the cows.

"*Mooo-mooo,*" bellowed the cows with a flick of their ears.

"*Ya-hoo!*" said Martin as he tried to count their spots.

They passed fields of corn and wheat. A farmer rode
by on his tractor leaving a dusty cloud behind him.

"*Choo-chooo,*" went the train as it flew past the fields.

"*Aaa-choo,*" sniffed the farmer as the dust tickled his nose.

"*Ya-hoo!*" said Martin spying a scarecrow in the corn.

Along came the conductor.

"Next stop is yours," he said to Martin with a smile.

The train slowed as it pulled into the station. Martin and his mother looked anxiously out the window.

"Yoo-hoo," shouted a lady with a big straw hat.

"Lu-Lu," squealed Martin's mother as she waved to her sister.

"Ya-hoo!" whooped Martin as he waved to his aunt.

"Ph-ew," said the engineer as he pulled on the brakes.

"Ssshhhhh-ssshhhhhh," went the train as it stopped with a sigh.

Manfred Meets the Tooth Monster

Written by Curtis Parkinson
Illustrated by Glen Mullaly

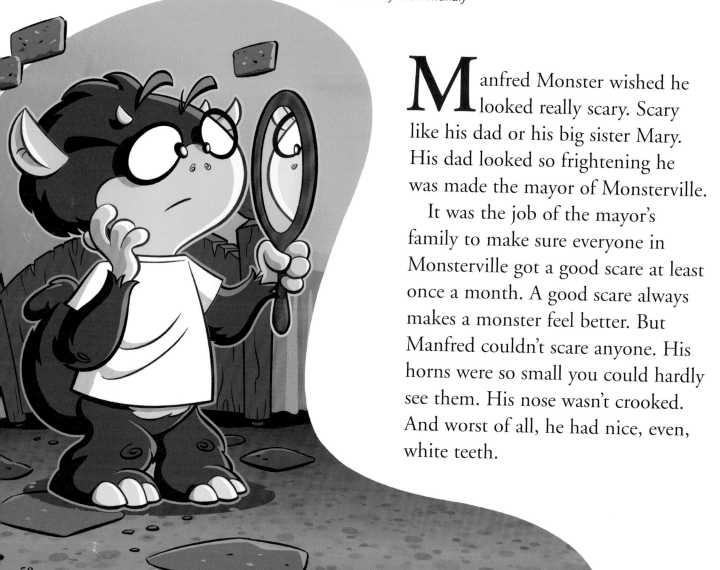

Manfred Monster wished he looked really scary. Scary like his dad or his big sister Mary. His dad looked so frightening he was made the mayor of Monsterville.

It was the job of the mayor's family to make sure everyone in Monsterville got a good scare at least once a month. A good scare always makes a monster feel better. But Manfred couldn't scare anyone. His horns were so small you could hardly see them. His nose wasn't crooked. And worst of all, he had nice, even, white teeth.

Still, Manfred tried his best to be a scary monster. He hid under Martha Monster's bed and jumped out just like he'd learned in monster school. But she only yawned and went back to sleep.

The other kid monsters weren't afraid of him either and invited him to play Hide-and-Shriek or Pin the Tail on the Dragon.

"I'm just no good at scaring," Manfred sighed.

One day, Manfred found that two of his front teeth were loose. He could wiggle them with his tongue. As he was getting ready for bed, they fell out.

"Put them under your pillow for the tooth monster," his mother said.

"What does the tooth monster do with the teeth?" Manfred asked.

"He collects them," his mother answered. "And he leaves something special for you in their place."

Manfred knew exactly what he wanted. And it wasn't a dime or even a quarter. But would he get it?

He brushed his teeth with his snail toothbrush and jumped into bed for his bedtime story, *Goldilocks and the Three Monsters*. As he fell asleep, he wondered if the tooth monster would really come.

In the middle of the night, Manfred heard a loud crash. The tooth monster had tripped over his stuffed octopus while sneaking out!

"Is this thing real?" the tooth monster grunted as he wrestled with the octopus.

Manfred felt under his pillow. There was something there, something hard and lumpy! The two teeth were gone. In their place was… a rock! A plain old rock!

The tooth monster, still tangled up with the octopus, saw the sad look on Manfred's face.

"Don't look so glum," he said. "It's a magic rock. You can turn it into anything you want."

"Magic? Thank you, tooth monster!" Manfred said.

"Just don't tell anyone you saw me," said the tooth monster, "or I'm in trouble."

And with that, he threw off the octopus, lurched to the window, and flew away, just missing the tree in the front yard.

Then Manfred rubbed the magic rock and made his wish.

And the next time he jumped out of a closet, the other kid monsters let out a very loud *EEEEKKK!*

Manfred had two long fangs where his front teeth used to be! Now Manfred can scare anyone in Monsterville.

But some of the braver kids still invite him to come over and play. They seem to know that Manfred, fangs and all, is really a nice monster inside.

What Should a Polar Bear Wear?

Written and Illustrated by Mélanie Watt

When it snows, Polo, Paula, and Pete rush to the window. They each know exactly how they want to spend a snowy day.

Polo wants to ski down the snow hill.

Paula wants to make snow angels.

Pete wants to build a snow bear.

But what should a polar bear wear? It's chilly outside, so they need to dress in warm clothes.

"I know what I want to wear!" says POLO the first polar bear. He chooses a hat, mittens, a scarf, and a pair of ski boots out of the BOX. Now he's ready to ski.

"I know what I want to wear!" says PAULA the second polar bear. She picks a purple hat, purple polka-dot mittens, a purple scarf, and a pair of purple boots out of the BOX. Now she's ready to make snow angels.

"But what should I wear?" asks  the third polar bear. PETE

He empties the Winter Clothes BOX onto the living room rug. He sees

a funny hat, earmuffs, four mittens, two scarves, and a

pair of boots.

Pete chooses the earmuffs instead of the funny hat...

He puts on the green mittens and picks out a scarf...

Then he slips on the pair of boots. Now he's ready to make a snow bear!

"I know what my snow bear will wear!" shouts as he hurries out the door. PETE

56

Outside, the three polar bears

play happily in the snow.

POLO skis down the snow hill.

PAULA makes snow angels.

And PETE dresses up his funny-looking snow bear.

What a warm and cozy way to spend a chilly, snowy day! 🐾

ABOUT THE COLLECTION

It was my great pleasure to work with Editor Katherine Dearlove to select stories originally published in *Chirp Magazine* for the *Animal Tales* collection. We had the challenging task of showcasing only a few of the talented writers and illustrators who have contributed to *Chirp* over the years.

While the stories are all delightful in their own right, they've been chosen to offer children a wide range of experiences with language and art. Fanciful tales like David McPhail's "Frank the Bear" and Maryann Kovalski's "Musical Mice" transport readers to other worlds. Mélanie Watt's charming rebus "What Should a Polar Bear Wear?" makes readers an integral part of the story. Roslyn Schwartz's whimsical watercolours in "Spike and Fluffy Get Dressed Up" perfectly complement her careful prose. And Clyde Henry's enchanting 3-D maquettes enhance Celia Barker Lottridge's classic bedtime tale.

The magic of *Animal Tales* — and the reason children will come back to it again and again — is in the unique ways the stories are told. Readers embark on voyages of discovery with the characters through the infectious rhythm of Jane Barclay's text and Rogé's playful illustrations in "Martin Takes the Train," and through the delicate textures of Marthe Jocelyn's paper sculputures in "Little Koi." Sharon Jennings and Ruth Ohi use gentle realism in "First Day Back" to explore the challenges of growing up. In "Armadillo's Special Day," Margriet Ruurs and Fil et Julie explore similar themes through fantastical humour.

Our sincere thanks to all of the wonderful writers and illustrators who have shared their craft and creativity in this collection. I hope you and your children have as much fun reading *Animal Tales* as I've had working on it.

Mary Beth

Mary Beth Leatherdale
Editorial Director, Owlkids

ABOUT THE AUTHORS & ILLUSTRATORS

Marie-Louise Gay has received eight nominations for the Governor General's Award for Illustration, winning for the books *Rainy Day Magic* (1987) and *Yuck, a Love Story* (2000). Based in Montreal, she writes books in French and English, and her books have been translated into twenty languages. Her latest works are *Stella, Princess of the Sky* and *Caramba,* which won the Marilyn Baillie Picture Book Award (2006). She also recently illustrated the book *Please Louise.*

Margriet Ruurs is the author of *Wake Up, Henry Rooster,* and *Emma's Cold Day.* She speaks at schools and conferences around North America and has a master's degree in education. Her most recent book is *In My Backyard.* Although Canadian, she currently lives in Shedd, Oregon.

Fil et Julie have worked as an illustration team since 1998 and are favourite contributors to *Chirp Magazine.* They also illustrated the Owlkids books *A Grandmother for Christmas, Annie Bizzanni,* and *Time for Bed.* Both have a background in graphic design. Fil studied animation and Julie studied visual arts.

David McPhail is the acclaimed author and illustrator of many books for children including *Pig Pig Grows Up* and *Lost!* He was awarded the *New York Times Book Review* Best Illustrated Book of the Year for *Mole Music* (1999). David currently lives in New Hampshire.

Marthe Jocelyn received the TD Canadian Children's Literature Award for *Mable Riley* (2005) and was nominated for the Governor General's Literary Award for Illustration for *Hannah's Collection* (2000). Born in Toronto, she is currently living in New York City. Her most recent book is *How it Happened in Peach Hill*.

Shawn Benjamin works in the daily television news department of the CBC. He has written several poems for *Chirp Magazine*. His poem "Tour the Town with Stacy the Taxi" was nominated for an Association of Educational Publishers award in 2004. He lives in Toronto.

Holli Conger is a digital and dimensional illustrator based in Nashville, Tennessee. She has a bachelor's degree in graphic design and advertising, and has illustrated magazines, CD covers, and children's books. Her most recent book is *Don't Touch, It's Hot*.

Roslyn Schwartz is the author and illustrator of the beloved *Mole Sisters* books, which have been adapted as a TV series. She also has two animated films with the National Film Board of Canada, one of which is for kids (*Arkelope*). Her most recent book is *Tales From Parc la Fontaine*. Roslyn lives in Montreal.

ABOUT THE AUTHORS & ILLUSTRATORS

Gary Barwin is the author of the picture books *Racing Worm Brothers* and *The Magic Mustache*. His young adult novel *Seeing Stars* was shortlisted for the Arthur Ellis Award for crime writing and the Canadian Library Association's Book Award. He lives in Hamilton, Ontario, where he teaches music at Hillfield Strathallan College.

Renée Mansfield illustrates for magazines, textbooks, television, and advertising. She makes her home in the Toronto area, where she teaches high school visual arts and communications technology.

Celia Barker Lottridge is the author of books for children of all ages and a storyteller who has performed in schools and libraries across Canada. Her story collection *Ten Small Tales* won an IODE Book Award in 1993. Her most recent book for younger children is *Berta: A Remarkable Dog*.

Clyde Henry Productions specializes in multimedia, stop-motion animation, and visual effects. Their National Film Board–produced film *Madame Tutli-Putli* won the Petit Rail d'Or and Canal+ Award for best short film at Cannes in 2007. Clyde Henry Productions is the nom de plume of artists Maciek Szczerbowski and Chris Lavis.

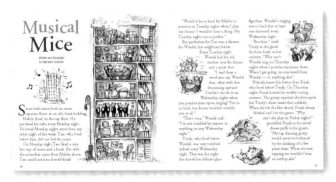

Maryann Kovalski received a Governor General's Literary Award for Illustration nomination for *The Big Storm* (1992) and has illustrated the books *Morning Glory Monday* and *Who is Your Favorite Monster, Mama?* She studied at the School of Visual Arts in New York City and currently divides her time between Toronto and New York.

Sharon Jennings is the author of *No Monsters Here* and *Bearcub and Mama*, which was a finalist for the Marilyn Baillie Picture Book Award (2006). She holds a master's degree in English from York University and currently lives in Toronto.

Ruth Ohi has illustrated more than forty children's books. She has also authored several including *A Trip with Grandma* and *The Couch Was a Castle*, an Amelia Frances Howard-Gibbon Award finalist (2007). Growing up in Bramalea, Ontario, she graduated from the Ontario College of Art. She lives in Toronto.

Eugenie Fernandes received a Governor General's Literary Award for Illustration nomination for the book *Earth Magic* (2006). She studied at the School of Visual Arts in New York City and lives in Peterborough, Ontario. Her husband Henry, and children Kim and Matthew, are also authors and illustrators.

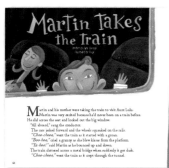

Jane Barclay received the Mr. Christie's Book Award Silver Seal for *Going on a Journey to the Sea* (2002) and *How Cold Was It?* (2000), which also won The Writers' Union of Canada's Writing for Children Competition. A native of Montreal, she also wrote *How Hot Was It?*, a Blue Spruce Award nominee in 2004.

Rogé received the Governor General's Literary Award for Children's Illustration for the book *Le gros monstre qui aimait trop lire* (2006). His pictures have been seen on many ad campaigns, posters, magazines, and in several children's picture books. Rogé studied graphic design at Laval University and now makes his home in Montreal.

Curtis Parkinson is a former chemical engineer who lives near Algonquin Park in Ontario. He is the author of *Mr. Reez's Sneezes* and *Tom Foolery*. His novel *Domenic's War* was shortlisted for a Silver Birch Award (2007) and his novel *Sea Chase* was nominated for a Red Cedar Book Award (2006-07). His most recent work is *Death In Kingsport*.

Glen Mullaly is an award-winning author and illustrator whose art often appears on the pages of *OWL*, *chickaDEE*, and *Chirp Magazine*s. He has illustrated more than sixty kids' books and 125 kids' book covers. Glen makes his home on Canada's West Coast and can be found online at www.glenmullaly.com.

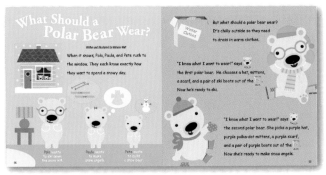

Mélanie Watt is the author and illustrator of *Leon the Chameleon*, *Augustine*, and *Scaredy Squirrel*, which won the Cybils Award in 2006, and the Blue Spruce Award, the Ruth and Sylvia Schwartz Children's Book Award, and the Amelia Frances Howard-Gibbon Illustrator's Award in 2007. A resident of Quebec, Mélanie studied design at the University of Quebec in Montreal. Her most recent book is *Chester*.